Words to Know Before You Read

announce

approach

demand

exclaim

gasp

middle

pitch

prance

respond

www.rourkeeducationalmedia.com

Edited by Precious McKenzie
Illustrated by Anita DuFalla
Art Direction and Page Layout by Renee Brady

Library of Congress PCN Data

Who's Right / Lin Picou
ISBN 978-1-61810-190-7 (hard cover) (alk. paper)
ISBN 978-1-61810-323-9 (soft cover)
Library of Congress Control Number: 2012936790

Rourke Educational Media
Printed in the United States of America,
North Mankato, Minnesota

rourkeeducationalmedia.com

customerservice@rourkeeducationalmedia.com • PO Box 643328 Vero Beach, Florida 32964

Who's Right

By Lin Picou

Illustrated by Anita DuFalla

"Let's play Duck, Duck, Goose!"
demands Priscilla Pony.

"We can't play that with only two of us!" says Lucy Goose.

"What should we do?" asks Lucy.

"We need to ask our friends to play with us,"
yells Priscilla as they run onto the playground.

6

"Hey, Mike Monkey, will you play Duck, Duck, Goose with us?"

"No, my brother and I like swinging from the monkey bars," responds Mike.

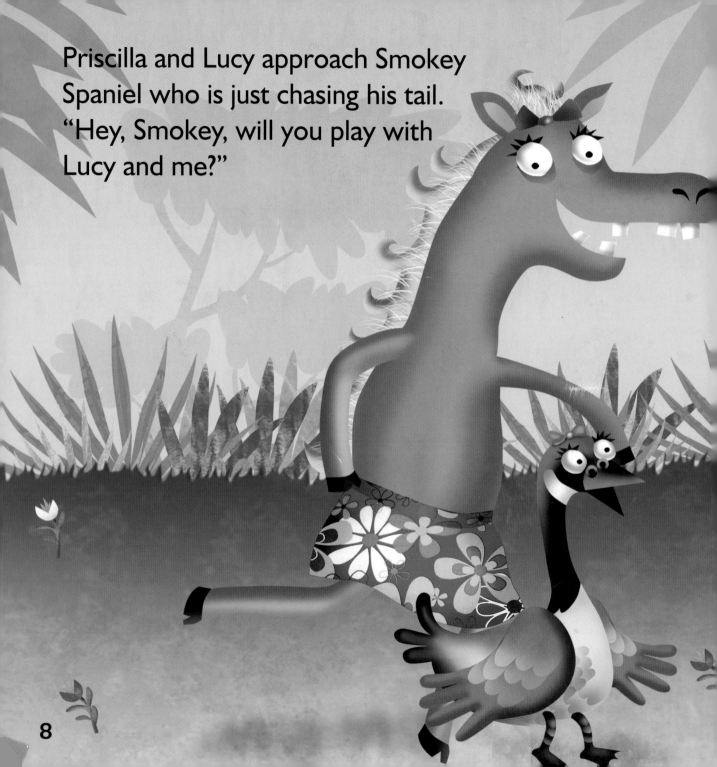

Priscilla and Lucy approach Smokey Spaniel who is just chasing his tail. "Hey, Smokey, will you play with Lucy and me?"

8

"Sorry, but I'm busy getting dizzy!" gasps Smokey.

Lucy runs to Ernest Elephant who is pitching a ball to Shirley Squirrel. "Will you play Duck, Duck, Goose with Priscilla and me?"

Shirley exclaims, "We're in the middle of a game here! Go ask someone else!"

11

Tallulah Turtle is racing Abby Gator when Priscilla approaches her. "Hey, slow down Tallulah, and join us for a game of Duck, Duck, Goose."

"I plan to win this race," shouts Abby Gator. "Don't get in our way, Priscilla!"

13

"O.K.," sighs Lucy Goose. "We need a plan."

Priscilla thinks and thinks. "How about if we ask Calypso Cat and Cooper Cub to play? We've never played with them before but maybe we can make some new friends."

14

"Hi, Cooper and Calypso. My name is Priscilla and this is Lucy. We want to play Duck, Duck, Goose, but we need more friends to make a circle."

"It's nice to meet you. You'll have to teach us the game because we always like to play Freeze Tag when we're on the playground."

"Well," explains Lucy, "everyone takes turns walking around a circle of friends, touching someone's head to be the duck."

"No, you're wrong, Lucy!" interrupts Priscilla. "First, you all sit in a circle while I walk around the outside of the circle, tapping your heads, saying, 'duck, duck, goose!' When I name a goose, the goose tries to tag me before I return to the empty spot in the circle."

18

"Who's right?" asks Cooper.
"Who knows?" shrugs Calypso.
"I am," shouts Lucy.
"Of course, I am," shouts Priscilla.

The new friends form a circle as Priscilla prances around them. "Duck, duck, goose!" She chooses Lucy as the goose.

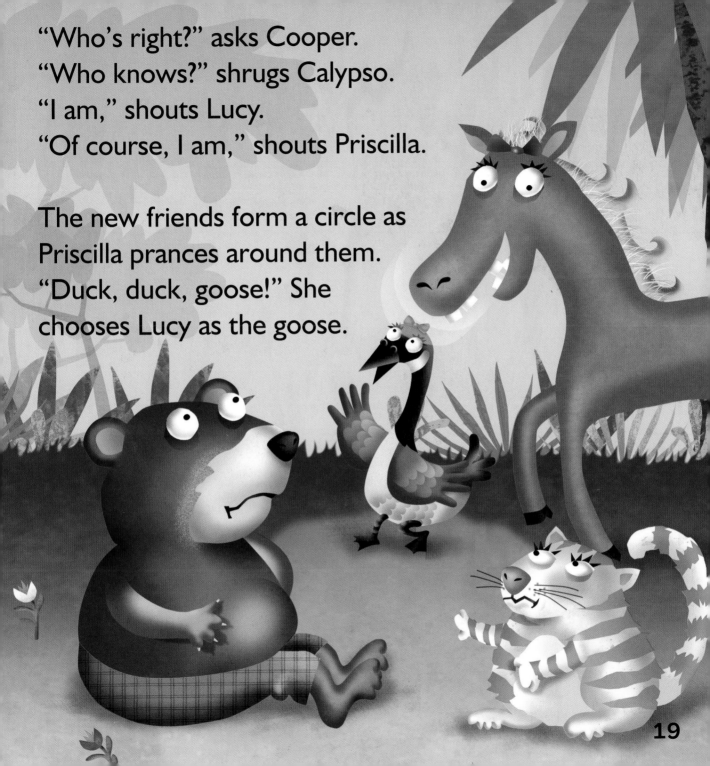

Lucy chooses Priscilla and Priscilla chooses Lucy. Then Lucy chooses Priscilla again and Priscilla chooses Lucy again.

Cooper Cub jumps up announcing,
"I'd rather play Freeze Tag with Calypso."
Lucy wonders, "Why don't they want to
play with us anymore?"

After Reading Activities

You and the Story...

Were Priscilla Pony and Lucy Goose right to invite friends to play with them and then not pick them as the goose in the game?

Were Calypso and Cooper right to leave the game without letting their new friends know why they were bored with Duck, Duck, Goose?

Words You Know Now...

Change the following verbs, or action words, to their past tenses by adding "ed," or "d."

announce   gasp

approach   pitch

demand   prance

exclaim   respond

You Could...Play Your Own Game

- Create a new hopscotch game using sidewalk chalk on a sidewalk or driveway.

- Try changing the traditional game of 10 squares in a row that alternates one square, double squares, one square, double squares, etc. by using triangles or circles.

- Try using a different pattern with the first hop being a double.

- Draw the hopscotch to 15 or 20 instead of stopping at 10. You can count by two's or five's when you write the numbers in each shape.

- Hop it sideways or on tiptoe. Draw hopscotches side by side, so you can race with a friend.

- Make a circular pattern with no end!

- Use a rock, shell, stick, or beanbag to throw into each shape being careful not to step into any shape with an object in it. The first player to throw a playing piece into each shape one at a time then hop the course, picking up that object on the way back, wins!

About the Author

Lin Picou spends time outside with her students every day playing golf, badminton, basketball, or catch. Her favorites include obstacle courses, bowling, and races. Recess helps us learn!

Ask The Author!
www.rem4students.com

About the Illustrator

Acclaimed for its versatility in style, Anita DuFalla's work has appeared in many educational books, newspaper articles, and business advertisements and on numerous posters, book and magazine covers, and even giftwraps. Anita's passion for pattern is evident in both her artwork and her collection of 400 patterned tights. She lives in the Friendship neighborhood of Pittsburgh, Pennsylvania with her son, Lucas.